As the *Galerider* descended through the clouds, Quint caught flashing glimpses of the rocky landscape below; vast, glistening grey slabs with jagged fissures between them. And there, where the sulphurous mist thinned for a moment, was the tall mast of another great sky pirate ship slicing through the gloom.

'We're not the first,' Quint shouted to his father.

'Nor shall we be the last,' Wind Jackal replied. 'A great pirate armada is gathering. It can mean only one thing.'

'What?' Quint asked.

'A sky battle,' his father replied simply . . .

Cloud Wolf is a dramatic adventure set in the world of *The Edge Chronicles*.

Specially published for World Book Day 2001

Also available in *The Edge Chronicles*,
by Paul Stewart and Chris Riddell,
published by Doubleday/Corgi Books:

BEYOND THE DEEPWOODS
STORMCHASER
MIDNIGHT OVER SANTAPHRAX

Praise for *The Edge Chronicles*:

'In the Tolkien/Pratchett tradition, fabulously illustrated and written with more than usual elegance' *The Sunday Times*

'Every single chapter of *Beyond the Deepwoods* is packed with action and adventure. There is a touch of the Lewis Carrolls to its authors' enthusiastic and uninhibited inventiveness and to the illustrations' *Starburst*

'The writing is so full of zest, Stewart's imagination is so fertile, his love of language so inventive that I maintain every child from 9 to 11 should be given a copy' *Interzone*

'Chris Riddell's superb illustrations are part and parcel of Paul Stewart's excellent fantasy series, *The Edge Chronicles*. The second, *Stormchaser*, is as action-packed as its predecessor' *Guardian*

'The story and the vast array of characters are captivating ... This is more than a read: it kidnaps and transports the reader' *School Librarian*

'For children who've read the Harry Potter books and want another world to explore ... Just fantasy and adventure, and wonderful line drawings' *Mail on Sunday*

'Fairly zips along ... gorgeous ink drawings ... bring on the next' *Observer*

And praise from some readers . . .

'*Beyond the Deepwoods* is a fantastic book full of enchantments and adventure with brilliant illustrations and a magical storyline . . . I have recommended the book to many of my friends and they have thought exactly the same' *Tom, East Sussex*

'Absolutely brilliant! . . . I couldn't put them down!' *Lin-May, Surrey*

'It was so good I was going on and on about how good it is and now my English teacher wants to read it' *reader in Wales*

'In the stories, your imaginative and colourful creatures, tribes and mystic characters really set my imagination alight . . . I really enjoyed the books and illustrations and can't wait to read the next book' *Andrew, Warwickshire*

'I loved your books even though I am dyslexic . . . I cannot wait for the next one to come out' *Johnnie, Richmond, London*

'I am writing to tell you about my love for your books in the Edge Chronicles series. My favourite character is the Banderbear and the Stone Pilot comes in second' *James, West Sussex*

'It has wonderful drawings and the story is fantastic . . . it was so good I read it at play and lunch-times at school!' *Rachel, High Wycombe*

'Once you start reading you can't put the book down' *reader in Wrexham*

'The book is one of the best I have ever read . . . you must buy this book; it has wonderful twists and a great ending' *reader in Wales*

For more information about the other titles in The Edge Chronicles, see details at the end of this book or check out the Transworld website on

www.**booksattransworld**.co.uk/childrens

THE DEEP WOODS

THE TWILIGHT WOODS

THE EDGELANDS

The Edge.

For William, Joseph, Anna, Katy and Jack

CLOUD WOLF
A CORGI BOOK : 0 552 547492

First publication in Great Britain

PRINTING HISTORY
Corgi edition published 2001, specially for World Book Day 2001

1 3 5 7 9 10 8 6 4 2

Set in 10½/15pt Bembo by Falcon Oast Graphic Art

Corgi Books are published by Transworld Publishers,
61–63 Uxbridge Road, London W5 5SA,
a division of The Random House Group Ltd,
in Australia by Random House Australia (Pty) Ltd,
20 Alfred Street, Milsons Point, Sydney, NSW 2061, Australia,
in New Zealand by Random House New Zealand Ltd,
18 Poland Road, Glenfield, Auckland 10, New Zealand
and in South Africa by Random House (Pty) Ltd,
Endulini, 5a Jubilee Road, Parktown 2193, South Africa

Made and printed in Great Britain by
Cox & Wyman Ltd, Reading, Berkshire.

CLOUD WOLF

THE EDGE CHRONICLES

Paul Stewart & Chris Riddell

CORGI BOOKS

Special publication for World Book Day 2001

Nana

Adu-offeh

INTRODUCTION

Far far away, jutting out into the emptiness beyond, like the figurehead of a mighty stone ship, is the Edge. There are many who inhabit its various landscapes; from the trolls, trogs and goblins of the perilous Deepwoods, to the phantasms and spectres of the treacherous Twilight Woods. The main town is Undertown, a seething urban sprawl which straddles the Edgewater River. Above it – fixed in position by the great Anchor Chain – is the floating city of Sanctaphrax, home to the academics.

In the distant history of the Edge, the only battles recorded arose from land disputes. This changed when the first Deepwoods explorers stumbled across the Stone Gardens and discovered the buoyant rocks which, used as flight-rocks, were to make skysailing possible. Today, it is up in the sky that the greatest Edge battles take place.

The first to take to the air in the new skyboats, were bird-catchers, small traders and some of the more fashionable families. Yet as Undertown grew bigger by the day, the sky was soon thronging with merchants in their barges and tugs bringing in all manner of Deepwoods produce; from food and drink, to textiles and timber.

As time passed, individual merchants started to group together, partly for mutual protection, partly to fix prices. Before long, there were dozens of them – leagues for every type of trade. Eventually, their leaders signed the notorious Alliance Treaty and formed the League of Undertown Free Merchants.

From this moment on, no business could exist and no trade could take place without going through the leagues – and the cost of the goods they handled rocketed. Many went hungry while the greedy leaguesmen grew fat.

The origins of the sky pirates, in contrast, are shrouded in mystery and romance. Some say that Wind Bear – a giant of an individual dispossessed by his Leaguesmaster brother – was the first sky pirate; that he waged war on the leagues out of revenge. Others claim that Little Jode, a humble tallow-trader, was the first to assemble a pirate-crew and take to the sky, in an attempt to undercut the crippling prices the leagues were demanding for candles.

What is certain is that the sky pirates opened up the skies again. They bought and sold cheaply, dealing directly with Deepwooders, Undertowners and Sanctaphrax academics – and cutting out the leaguesmen in the middle. And, when the opportunity arose, they were not above attacking the infamous league ships – run by corrupt tyrants and crewed by slave labour – relieving them of their cargo and distributing it to those in need.

The sky pirates became folk heroes and the stories of their exploits were told far and wide. There are several tales about Wind Bear, and Little Jode, but none more than about Cloud Wolf, whom many believe was the finest sky pirate captain that ever lived.

What follows is but one of those tales.

. CHAPTER ONE .

WILDERNESS LAIR

'Prepare for descent, Ramrock,' Wind Jackal called to his stone pilot. His hands ran expertly over the bone-handled levers, tweaking the sails and adjusting the hull-weights. 'We're going down.'

'Aye-aye, captain,' Ramrock shouted back. Clad in the characteristic stone-pilot garb – a thick hooded coat and heavy boots – he worked calmly to raise the temperature of the rock. The torches flared as he pulled the heating lever, the bellows blew the scorched air into the stone cage and, as the rock within began to glow, so the *Galerider* began to descend.

Quint looked over the balustrade of the sky pirate ship and shuddered. Was his father mad? the youth wondered. Going down *there*, into the Edgelands!

Situated between the Deepwoods and the yawning abyss beyond the Edge, the Edgelands was an inhospitable rocky wasteland, swirling with thick, treacherous mists, where spirits and nightmares

13

shrieked and howled, and the gloamglozer – the wickedest creature in all the Edge – was said to dwell.

Quint crossed to the helm. 'Is this wise, Father?' he said.

'Steady on the boom, Master Queep!' Wind Jackal bellowed back along the sky ship to his quarter-master. 'Grappling-hooks at the ready!' He glanced round at his son. 'Wise?' he said.

'I thought we were heading for Sanctaphrax,' said Quint. 'You told me the Most High Academe had requested an audience.'

'He has,' said Wind Jackal. 'But something else has come up. Something far too big to be ignored.'

'Father?' said Quint.

'A carrier-ratbird arrived last night bearing a message from Ice Fox . . .' The storm winds buffeted the side of the sky ship with ferocious force. Wind Jackal lowered the neben-hull-weights to compensate. 'A sky-pirate assembly has been called for this evening,' he continued, 'away from prying eyes, here at Wilderness Lair. And I don't have to tell you how unusual that is, Quint. The old skycur must be on to something big.'

'But what about the Most High Academe?' Quint asked.

'Sky willing we'll complete our business and be back in Sanctaphrax in time to keep our

appointment,' said Wind Jackal. 'And if we are not; well, Linius Pallitax and I go back a long way, and what is half a day between old friends?' He peered down. 'Lower the mainsail!' he boomed. 'Furl the jib!'

Quint shrugged and returned to the balustrade.

As the *Galerider* descended through the clouds, Quint caught flashing glimpses of the rocky landscape below; vast glistening grey slabs with jagged fissures between them. And there, where the sulphurous mist thinned for a moment, was the tall mast of another great sky pirate ship slicing through the gloom.

'We're not the first,' Quint shouted to his father.

'Nor shall we be the last,' Wind Jackal replied. 'A great pirate armada is gathering. It can mean only one thing.'

'What?' Quint asked.

'A sky battle,' his father replied simply.

Wilderness Lair was not so much situated *in* the Edgelands as *beneath* it. Through the gaps in the mist, Quint could see other sky pirate ships coming in from all directions and sailing over the jutting lip of rock. As Wind Jackal followed them, Quint gasped as the *Galerider* was suddenly battered by the full strength of the incoming storms.

Slowly, carefully, his father brought the sky ship round and headed back towards the cliff-face. Beneath the overhang, Quint saw a dozen or more sky pirate ships clinging to the sheer rock. He held his breath as the sky ship dipped sharply in the sky and threatened to roll. The wind howled. The mist swirled. The rockface came closer.

'Fire the fasting-spikes!' Wind Jackal bellowed. 'Launch the grappling-hooks!'

A volley of metal shot through the air and landed with muffled thuds and clangs. Some fell away, but others held firm. The sky pirates tugged at the ropes and secured them tightly. The *Galerider* came to rest alongside the other sky ships. Together, they clung to the vertical cliff-face like a cluster of rock-limpets.

Quint sighed with relief and glanced round. 'Look!' he shouted and pointed to his left. 'It's the *Fogscythe*! And the *Mistmarcher*.' He turned the other way. 'And there's the *Windspinner*.'

His heart swelled with pride to see how many had come from all corners of the Edge in answer to Ice Fox's call. Loners, sky pirates might be, but when the need arose, they would band together like no-one else.

Each sky ship was distinct from its neighbour, depending on the fighting techniques favoured by the individual captains. The *Fogscythe* was fitted with curved fore-blades which could slice through the sails and rigging of enemy ships; while the elegant *Windspinner* had, fixed to its aftcastle, an intricate catapult that hurled molten pitch onto an opponent's flight rock to send the ship into a spiralling descent.

'And look,' said Wind Jackal, nodding towards a two-mast vessel with a great brass harpoon at its prow. 'It's the *Cloudbreaker*. Ice Fox himself must already be here.'

The moment the *Galerider* moored, sky pirates from the adjacent ships lowered gangplanks and rope-bridges both to connect the fleet and to allow access, one with the other – for those daring enough to brave the flimsy walkways in such weather. Soon the *Galerider*, like all the other sky pirate ships in the growing fleet, was bustling with activity.

Old friends greeted one another warmly. Acquaintances were rekindled. Stories were swapped. And as more and more sky pirate ships broke through the cloud cover and attached themselves to the cliff-face, so the party-like atmosphere grew increasingly rowdy. Queep discovered that a long-lost cousin had become the *Mistmarcher*'s head cook, while Steg Jambles – a bluff, bearded character – went off in search of his old flat-head sparring partner, Hogmutt, who had been crewing on board the *Fogscythe* the last time he'd heard from him.

Quint, too, would have liked to explore the other ships. He wanted to meet Grist Greystone, the grizzled quartermaster of the *Fogscythe*, and talk to him about his role in the infamous ironwood blockade. He wanted to examine the catapult mechanism of the *Windspinner*. But Wind Jackal was adamant.

'You're to remain here where I can keep an eye on you,' he said.

'Oh, but Father,' Quint protested. 'I'm not a child any more. I can look after myself.'

'Quint, Quint,' chided Wind Jackal. 'Don't always be in such a hurry to grow up. Whatever you may think, there's still much you have to learn. Believe me.'

Quint nodded. 'Yes, Father,' he said irritably.

With the approaching darkness came the night-chorus of the Edgelands. Deep rumbling groans and low chattering drowned out the constant roar of the wind; shrill, blood-curdling cries set Quint's heart racing. Suddenly, staying on board the *Galerider* didn't seem such a bad idea after all, and he followed his father round as he lit the oil lamps and tallow lanterns.

All at once, a loud, almost mechanical, voice filled the air. It was Ice Fox. Everyone turned in the direction of the noise to see the sky pirate captain himself standing in the caternest of the *Cloudbreaker*, a megaphone raised to his lips. A second individual was standing beside him, head held high.

'My friends,' Ice Fox bellowed above the noise of the battering storm. 'Eighteen of you I summoned to Wilderness Lair. Eighteen sky pirate ships are here.' He paused. 'I have important news.'

The pirates stopped talking and listened closely.

'Undertown is a free city with free citizens,' said Ice Fox. 'It is written in the constitution that no-one is permitted to enslave another. Yet the leagues-men flout this law. They press-gang any they find to crew their ships – and kill those who refuse!'

There was a rumble of indignant murmuring.

'Who among us has not heard of the *Great Sky Whale*?'

The muttering grew louder. The *Great Sky Whale*, a vast four-mast league ship, was notorious throughout the Edge for the riches it transported – and the barbaric treatment of its crew.

'This youth,' Ice Fox continued, nodding to the gangly figure beside him, 'who, three days since, managed to escape from the *Great Sky Whale*, can bear witness to the terrible conditions on board. The ceaseless labour. The pitiful rations of food. The incessant beatings . . .' He looked round. 'An unimaginable existence for a sky pirate.'

'You can say that again!' someone shouted.

'Bloodsucking leaguesmen!' another cursed. 'Something should be done to teach them a lesson!'

'Something *will* be done,' Ice Fox broke in. 'For the news I bring is that the *Great Sky Whale* is currently travelling from the Deepwoods to Undertown, laden with jewels . . .'

'But the ship travels with the entire Hammerhead Goblin Guard on board,' a voice pointed out. 'And you know what they say about those hammerheads. Cruel, pitiless . . .'

'Fight to the death as soon as look at you!' added another.

'And what about the armed escort fleet?' asked a

third. 'Thirty league ships there were at the last count, all bristling with weapons . . .'

Ice Fox raised his hands for quiet. 'I have information that for this trip the *Great Sky Whale* is travelling without an escort fleet and with only a single hammerhead guard company on board.' A hush descended. 'Apparently, the Leaguesmaster, Marl Mankroyd, has commissioned the boat . . .'

A ripple of anger went round. The Leaguesmaster's reputation went before him.

'. . . unbeknown to the other leaguesmen,' he went on. 'You know how treacherous they can be, even among themselves. He has just completed an illicit jewel deal with the glintergoblins of the Northern Mines and the *Great Sky Whale* is carrying a small, but priceless, cargo of black diamonds. Mankroyd was hoping to feather his own nest without any other leaguesmen finding out. But with no escort fleet, and but a single company of the hammerhead guard,' he said, spelling it out, 'we shall pluck the treasure out from under his nose!'

A roar of approval went up.

'And we will free the captive crew.'

The roar grew louder.

'We will destroy the evil slave vessel once and for all!'

Ice Fox's words were drowned out completely by the shouting of the sky pirates. Quint turned – a

22

broad grin plastered across his face – to see his father looking oddly sombre.

'Who is this youth that brings such unexpected tidings?' Wind Jackal called across to Ice Fox.

'This is Pen,' Ice Fox replied, and raised his arm high in the air. 'Former bootspit to the Leaguesmaster himself. Now, a freeman once more.'

'Pen . . . Pen . . .' Wind Jackal murmured thoughtfully. The name was unfamiliar – yet the face of the gangly youth with the huge hands and feet was not. Where had he seen him before? He shook his head.

'We shall depart for the Deepwoods at daybreak,' Ice Fox continued. 'We shall use ratbirds to track the *Great Sky Whale* in the vastness of the Deepwoods. When they find it, we must strike as one, for even without its escort ships, the *Great Sky Whale* is still the most formidable of all league ships. But we shall overpower it by force of numbers.' He paused and looked round. 'And when we do, the treasure of the *Great Sky Whale* will be ours!'

A tumultuous cheer – the loudest so far – went up. They could do it. They *would* do it!

. CHAPTER TWO .

RATBIRDS AND TURBULENT-FOG

Quint barely slept a wink that night. He lay in his hammock, tossing and turning with excitement. He would be first on board the *Sky Whale*. He would be brave and resourceful. He would make his father proud.

With such thoughts he drifted off to sleep, only to be woken a moment later by the sounds of the Edgelands themselves – for this was a forsaken place. The vast cliff-face fell away into blackness, with cloud banks breaking against it like raging waves. The mists and clinging fog swirled ceaselessly, conjuring up strange apparitions and ghoulish faces, while the winds howled and whistled through the cracks and crevices of the rock; a ghastly chorus of wailing shrieks and anguished cries.

With a shudder, Quint pulled the covers up over his head, and turned his mind away from the unseen horrors out there, and back to the coming battle. His eyelids grew heavy . . .

'*Waaaa-iiiee!*' came a blood-curdling screech, and Quint was wide awake once again.

'What *is* that?' he wondered nervously.

And so it went on. All night. By sunrise Quint had already abandoned any attempt to sleep, and was dressed and ready. As the first patches of pink light dusted the sky, he went up on deck.

It was a chilly morning. The mist clung to him like wet clothes.

'Quint!' came Wind Jackal's surprised voice. 'You're up early.'

Quint turned to see his father in the misty shadows at the rear of the ship. Steg Jambles was with him. They were standing either side of a large cage, each holding a ratbird in his hands.

'I couldn't sleep,' he said.

'Too excited, eh, Master Quint?' said Steg. 'I know the feeling.'

Quint nodded. He didn't mention the grinding fear which had gripped him every time one of the spirits or ghouls – or whatever they were – had cried out.

'Odd-looking little things, ratbirds, aren't they?' he said to change the subject. He tickled one under the chin. 'How will they find their way?'

'I've taught them to seek and home,' Steg Jambles explained. 'They use sun-angle and wind-direction, plus they have an acute sense of smell. The scarf of that youth, Pen, has been cut up and distributed amongst all of us,' he said, removing a fragment of spotted cloth from his top pocket and rubbing it round the ratbird's snout. 'Its scent will guide the ratbirds to the great league ship. While this,' he said, passing a smooth musk-rock pebble back and forth across the cage door, 'will help them to return.' He threw the creature into the air. 'Now fly, rat-bird. Fly!'

The ratbird switched its tail, flapped its furry wings and, with a squeaky screech, was gone. Wind Jackal's ratbird flew after it, followed – in quick succession – by the half dozen others which had been waiting in the cage. The same procedure was being repeated on all the other sky pirate ships. And as the curious flying creatures were swallowed up by the dense, swirling mist, the sky pirates fingered the lucky charms around their necks and prayed for a swift and successful return.

'Now the ratbirds have gone, it is time for us also to set forth,' said Wind Jackal. 'Raise the gang-planks!' he bellowed. 'Unhitch the walkways. Prepare the flight-rock, Ramrock.' He took his place at the helm. 'Detach the fasting-spikes!'

The next moment, the *Galerider* and the rest of the sky pirate fleet soared into the sky like a great flock of winged raptors. Quint raised his head and shuddered with pleasure as the wind blew into his face. Skysailing! There was nothing in the world that came even close to the wonderful sensation of soaring across the sky.

'Quint!' Wind Jackal called out. 'Come and take the helm.'

Quint jumped to it eagerly. And while his father operated the bone-handled levers behind him, adjusting the sails, fine-tuning the hull-weights, Quint turned the great wheel this way, that way, feeling the sky ship responding to his touch like a wild and wilful creature. Far, far ahead – where the rocky Edgelands met the forest – he caught the first glimpse of the tallest treetops, tipped with silver and gold from the rising sun.

'The Deepwoods!' he exclaimed.

'Aye, lad, there they are,' said Wind Jackal. 'And somewhere above their sprawling vastness, the *Great Sky Whale* awaits.'

*

Several hours were to pass before the *Galerider* reached the Deepwoods, by which time the weather had deteriorated.

'Where are those ratbirds?' Wind Jackal muttered, as he scanned the horizon with his telescope.

Quint removed his own telescope and joined in the search. Apart from several of the other sky pirate ships – now widely spread out across the sky – the only airborne creature to be seen was a lone rotsucker, flapping across the sky with a sealed caterbird cocoon dangling from its taloned feet. The Deepwoods looked vast enough to conceal a hundred mighty league ships.

'What do we do?' Quint asked.

'We keep looking,' said Wind Jackal. 'And we remain patient.'

Midday came and went. Late afternoon turned to early evening. Quint scoured the horizon until his eyes hurt. Would they ever see the ratbirds again?

'Ratbirds on the starboard bow at two hundred strides,' shouted Spillins, the ageing oakelf lookout. 'Two of them . . . No, three.'

Wind Jackal bellowed for Steg Jambles. It was important that, as ratbird keeper, he be there on deck to see the aerial display put on by the birds when they reached the sky ship. For like woodbees, whose curious wiggle-dance informed the rest of the hive about a source of nectar, so the dips and dives of the ratbirds' flight would reveal the direction and distance of the object they had been sent out to seek.

'Ratbirds at fifty strides,' cried Spillins.

'Steg!' roared Wind Jackal for a second time. 'Where are you?'

'Here, captain,' came a breathless voice.

'The ratbirds are over there,' said Wind Jackal urgently.

'I see them,' said Steg. The ratbirds were getting closer. If they simply returned to their cages, then hunger had been their motive for returning. But if they performed their dance . . .

The three creatures flew once, twice, three times round the mast and suddenly soared back into the sky. 'Thank Sky for that,' Steg muttered. A moment later, and just as suddenly, they tumbled back down, turning somersaults as they dropped. With less than a stride to go before smashing into the deck, they pulled out of the dive and landed on top of the cage. Wind Jackal turned to Steg.

'How many somersaults did you count?' he asked.

'Twelve,' said Steg. He frowned thoughtfully and Quint watched his lips move as he made calculations. 'The *Great Sky Whale*,' he announced at last, 'is positioned at three degrees west of north-north-west.' He paused. 'At about twenty thousand strides off.'

Wind Jackal nodded. 'Which, with these winds, is a good night's travel away.' He turned to his son. 'You're looking exhausted, Quint,' he said. 'Go and get some sleep.'

'But, Father . . .' Quint protested.

'You won't miss any of the excitement,' his father said. 'I'll wake you the moment we catch sight of the *Sky Whale*. Now go.' He looked round. 'Steg,' he said. 'Take the helm.'

'Aye-aye, cap'n,' Steg replied.

Quint stood aside. He was far too tired to put up any resistance. His father was right. The previous night had left him fit for nothing. He really did need to get some sleep.

Down below deck, Quint climbed into his hammock. The cabin was quiet and dark, his covers were warm, and the gentle sway of flight was soothing. With the howls and shrieks of the Edgelands no more than a distant memory, Quint was asleep within seconds.

*

In the early dawn light, Wind Jackal paced the upper-deck thoughtfully. Steg was standing at the helm.

'That lanky youth with the big hands and feet,' Wind Jackal said. 'The one with Ice Fox – did you recognize him?'

Steg shook his head. 'Can't say as I did, captain. Why?'

'I'm not sure,' said Wind Jackal. 'There was something familiar about him.' He shuddered. 'Something I didn't like . . .' he said, and added; 'It's a good job Quint isn't around to hear his father prattling on like some superstitious old gabtroll.'

Steg looked at Wind Jackal evenly. 'Where I come from, we take such things seriously,' he said. 'My old grandma – Sky rest her spirit – reckoned that premonitions, intuition and the like, were all part of the "silent language". *Turn away, and rue the day*, that's what she used to say.'

'Turbulent-fog at four thousand strides, and rising,' Spillins' strident voice announced from the caternest.

Turbulent-fog rising! Both Wind Jackal and Steg looked round and recoiled in horror.

Normally, turbulent-fog was a low-sky phenomenon, seldom rising up much higher than the tops of the Deepwoods' trees and so, easy to fly over. But not this time. This time, the vast wall of fog which extended from horizon to horizon also towered far, far above the tree-line. Wind Jackal had to think quickly. In less than five minutes, the sky ship would be swallowed up.

Thick and viscous, yet as full of air-pockets as hammelhorn cheese, turbulent-fog was notorious. The sticky air played havoc with flight-rocks, blocking their porous surface, reducing buoyancy and causing them to sink. This would have been manageable if it hadn't been for the pockets of icy, crystal clear air trapped inside the fog, for each time a sky ship penetrated one of these, its flight-rock would 'breathe' again, and soar upwards. Many was the Undertown tug, barge and even unwary league ship that had been shaken to pieces in its violent down-pull and up-draft.

'Turbulent-fog at a thousand strides!' shrieked the oakelf.

'Sky protect us all,' Wind Jackal murmured as he pressed the amulets round his neck to his lips.

'Captain!' Steg Jambles cried out in alarm. 'What are we going to do?'

Wind Jackal reached out, gripped the bone-handled levers and breathed in deeply. 'We'll try to fly above it. Hang on tight, Steg. If we can't, it'll have to be a vertical rise!'

Steg gasped.

Wind Jackal lowered the stern-weights. He lifted the prow-weights and raised the sails. With a lurch and a sigh, the *Galerider* soared upwards. The wall of fog came closer. It was like scaling a mighty waterfall.

'Get ready to douse the flight-rock on my order, Ramrock!' he shouted to his stone pilot.

'Turbulent-fog at five hundred strides!'

'Come on, my lovely,' Wind Jackal urged the sky ship as, creaking and cracking, it rose higher and higher. 'You can do it!'

Above their heads, the top of the bank of fog came closer – but not before the *side* of the approaching wall.

'Impact in five seconds!' the oakelf called.

Wind Jackal's expert fingers raced over the rows of levers – raising here, lowering there. The sky ship rose more quickly.

'Four!'

'We're not going to make it,' shouted Steg.

'Three . . .'

'Douse the flight-rock!' Wind Jackal bellowed.

Ramrock pulled a lever. The flight-rock was instantly smothered with chilled earth. It groaned and creaked as it cooled. Immediately, the sky ship soared skywards, almost vertically and at break-neck speed. Despite their best efforts, however, there was nothing that either the captain or his stone pilot could do to evade the oncoming fog.

'Impact!' Spillins bellowed.

*

The instant it entered the sticky purple-grey fog, the *Galerider* stopped rising. The fog choked the porous flight-rock and the sky ship began a slow, shuddering descent. Neither Ramrock nor Wind Jackal could steady it.

The *Galerider* dropped through the dense, stickiness, gathering speed as it went. All of a sudden the fog disappeared and the sky ship hit its first big airpocket. The air was cold and crystal clear all round them.

'Rope yourselves down!' Wind Jackal bellowed to the crew-members up on deck, as he seized a tolley-rope of his own and tied it round his waist.

The pores in the surface of the rock expelled the claggy fog and sucked in the pure, clean air, causing the flight-rock itself to become abruptly super-buoyant. With a judder and a lurch, the sky ship rocketed up into the air as if fired from a mighty catapult. Terrified, the crew cried out and fell to the deck, clutching hold of anything they could find. Higher and higher the *Galerider* flew, right up to the top of the air-pocket – and back into the fog itself.

Immediately, the sky ship slowed down, and then began to sink once more. Steg Jambles and Ramrock both climbed to their feet. Wind Jackal lowered the sails. Down in his cabin below deck, Quint picked himself off the floor and looked round with surprise. One moment he'd been in his hammock

dreaming of how proud he'd just made his father, the next he was flying across the room.

He rubbed his eyes and tried to gather his thoughts. Had they found the *Great Sky Whale*? Were they about to attack? He frowned. 'Why didn't Father wake me? He promised he would!'

Quint slipped on his longcoat and parawings, checked that his knife was on his belt and left the room. As he hurried up the stairs the sky ship juddered violently. Below him, he heard the frantic screeching and squawking of the ratbirds which lived in the bowels of the ship. The next moment . . . *FWOOOPFF!* The *Galerider* was rocketing upwards for a second time.

Quint fell to his knees and gripped the rope-banister with both hands. His stomach heaved. His head spun. 'What's happening?' he groaned. 'I've never known it so rough before.'

CHAPTER THREE .

ATTACK!

'The ship won't take much more of this, captain,' Steg Jambles moaned as the *Galerider* came out of an ascent, travelling so fast and reaching so high that old Spillins up in the caternest had actually blacked out.

'Steady, old friend,' Wind Jackal replied, as he realigned the port hull-weights. 'The fog's thinning.'

The rest of the fleet was nowhere to be seen. Had they escaped the terrible fog? Wind Jackal could only pray that they had. Steg Jambles squinted ahead. 'We do seem to be dropping less quickly,' he said.

'Father, what in Sky's name is going on?' came a voice.

Wind Jackal turned. 'Quint!' he said. 'I thought you were safely tucked up in your hammock.'

'What, with all this upping and downing?' said Quint.

'Hold on tight,' said Wind Jackal through clenched teeth. 'It's not over yet.'

They hit another air-pocket. The *Galerider* listed sharply to one side and surged upwards. Quint fell to the floor, skidded across the deck and slammed into the fore-balustrade.

'Quint!' Wind Jackal bellowed.

'Grab this rope, Master Quint,' Steg Jambles shouted as he tossed the end in his direction.

Quint, who was clutching hold of the spindles of the balustrade, released one hand and seized the rope. He wound it round and round his arm and held on grimly. The upward force drained the blood from his head, making him giddy. He let go of the wooden spindle and slithered back down the sloping deck.

'Quint!' Wind Jackal cried out a second time. With the tolley-rope still tied around his own waist, he dived after his son. His hands grasped at a bony

38

ankle and held on tight. The rope went taut. Wind Jackal tightened his grip.

At that moment, the sky ship left the vast pocket of air and abruptly slowed down once more. The descent through the sticky fog began again. This time, however, something was different. Instead of gathering speed, the *Galerider* slowed until it was hovering at one height. Then it righted itself.

Wind Jackal lifted his head and looked round. The fog was thin and wispy; neither dense enough to make the flight-rock plummet, nor so crystal clear that it would exaggerate the stone's natural buoyancy.

'We made it,' he breathed. 'But at what cost?' He noticed the rigging, torn away from the masts and hanging limp; and the sails, some slightly torn, some completely shredded. 'Sky alone knows how many of the others have made it.' He shook his head. 'I fear you'll have to wait to experience your first sky battle, Quint.'

The great sky pirate fleet shattered? Quint could hardly believe it. He walked over to the side of the sky ship. Behind them the great wall of fog was receding. In front, the sky was becoming clearer with every passing second. He narrowed his eyes and squinted into the distance.

'Look!' he shouted excitedly. 'Over there.'

Wind Jackal raised his telescope and focused on the dark spot where Quint was pointing. 'It's probably just another rotsucker,' he said. 'Or a cater-bird. Or . . .' He paused. 'It's the *Fogscythe*!' he exclaimed.

'It is!' Quint cried triumphantly. 'And over there!' he said, swinging his outstretched arm around to the left. 'Is that the *Mistmarcher*? And beyond that a ways, that must be the *Windspinner*. Look, you can see the great catapult fixed to its aftcastle.'

Wind Jackal nodded. 'And not looking *too* much the worse for wear,' he said thoughtfully.

'Better still is what's above us,' said Steg Jambles.

'Above us?' said Quint.

Steg nodded up into the sky, high above their heads, where a sturdy craft in pristine condition was sailing across the sky with a further half dozen sky ships following behind in a V-shaped form-ation. They looked like a migrating skein of gullet-geese.

'That's the *Cloudbreaker* up in front!' Quint announced excitedly.

'So I see,' said Wind Jackal. 'Why, that wily old skycur, Ice Fox. He only managed to get above the turbulent-fog, didn't he?' He chuckled. 'He must have been up there the whole time, waiting to see how many of us got through.'

'They're signalling us,' said Steg, as a flashing light glinted from the *Cloudbreaker*.

Although loners, the sky pirates had several ways

of communicating with each other. And while ratbirds were used for long distances, reflective slivers
of silver marble were the chosen means of convey-
ing information over shorter stretches of sky.

'*League . . . ship . . at . . . north . . . west . . . four . . .
thousand . . . strides . . .*' Wind Jackal said, as the
message built up, letter by letter. '*Follow . . . us . . .*'
He turned to Quint. 'Looks like it's on again,' he
said.

Quint grinned. 'My first sky battle!'

By three thousand strides away from the league
ship, most of the sky pirate ships which had set off
from Wilderness Lair had formed themselves into a
fleet, headed by the *Cloudbreaker*.

The crew of the *Galerider* was getting ready. Up on
deck, Steg and Quint carried out makeshift repairs
to the rigging and sails. Spillins was hammering the
broken side-panels of his caternest back into place.
Grim and Grem, cloddertrog twins, were using their
enormous bulk to shift the great sky-harpoon back
into position; while Ratbit – a wiry, swivel-eyed
mobgnome – was down beneath the ship, checking
the rudder-wheel and hull-weights.

Below deck, Queep the quartermaster hurried
from stockroom to store, returning the spilled
supplies to their rightful places and tying everything down in preparation for the oncoming battle.

Ramrock was, as always, with his beloved flight-rock, venting and re-boring it as best he could.

'You need a full steam-irrigation,' he was muttering, 'and as soon as we return to Undertown, that's the first thing you'll get. But for the time being, this will have to do . . .'

At two thousand strides away from their destination, everyone on board the *Galerider* was ready. Wind Jackal locked the bone-handled flight levers in place and took Quint aside.

'There's something I must tell you,' he said.

Quint frowned. 'Father?' he said.

'I know you're excited,' he said. 'I remember how *I* felt when your grandfather took me on my first sky pirate raid – and that was a small affair compared with this . . .'

'I . . . I won't let you down,' said Quint. 'I'm going to make you proud of me . . .'

'I know you are, son,' said Wind Jackal warmly. 'Steg says you've volunteered for the advance boarding party. Is that true?'

'Yes, Father,' said Quint. 'I want to be there right from the start. I want to be first on board and . . .'

'No,' said Wind Jackal firmly. 'It's out of the question. The advance boarding party is made up of the toughest and most experienced pirates in the fleet. Grim and Grem from our sky ship; Hogmutt from the *Fogscythe* . . . It's no place for a first-timer.'

'But Father . . .'

'Sky above, Quint, don't you think *I'd* like to go in the first wave? But my place is here, with the *Galerider*. And your place is here next to me. Besides, have you any idea how brutal those hammerheads can be?' Then, seeing the look of disappointment on his son's face, his voice softened. 'You can go in with the second wave,' he said. 'With Steg and the others, when the hammerhead guards have been knocked out and it's safe. But only then. And only with my say-so. Is that understood?'

'But . . .'

'That's enough!' he snapped. 'You will do as I tell you!'

And Quint fell silent, knowing his father well enough to realize that if he uttered another word, he would not be allowed on the league ship at all. All the same, the decision hurt.

At a thousand strides, the look-out on board the *Cloudbreaker* spotted the *Great Sky Whale* for the first time. Word instantly went round the rest of the fleet. Quint raised his telescope to his eye.

'There it is!' he cried out excitedly.

'No mistaking it,' said Wind Jackal. 'It's the largest sky ship that's ever sailed. It must be at least ten times the size of the *Galerider*.'

Quint stared in awe. 'Four masts, four flight-rocks,

43

eight sky rafts. And a solid-gold figurehead . . .'

'Yes, and a company of fearsome hammerhead guards, don't forget,' Wind Jackal interrupted. 'So you mind what I told you.'

Quint nodded sullenly.

Despite its size and formidable array of weaponry, the *Great Sky Whale* was a cumbersome vessel; a ridiculous triumph of design over function. It was slow and notoriously awkward to sail – yet as a symbol of brute-force it was awe-inspiring. That, presumably, was why Marl Mankroyd had decided to use the ship in his gem-dealings. Now, with the fleet of swift, manoeuvrable sky pirate ships bearing heavily down on him, Wind Jackal, Ice Fox and the other sky pirate captains were all hoping that it was a decision he would live to regret.

As they approached the great looming league ship, the sky pirate ships fanned out. Then, at a given signal and using cloud-cover to conceal them whenever they could, they swooped in on gusting cross-winds. One by one, they surrounded the huge vessel – like woodwasps circling a hammel-horn – taking up pre-arranged positions and holding them.

Ice Fox surveyed the scene below him, a smile playing on his lips. There were no guards on the deck of the *Great Sky Whale*. Three of the four cater-nests were empty, while the look-out in the fourth

seemed to be asleep. The captain was nowhere to be seen. He was about to be punished for his complacency. Ice Fox nodded to his quartermaster, who in turn signalled to all of the watching, waiting sky pirates. The mirror flashed out a single word.

Attack.

With deft fingers, Wind Jackal lowered the prow-weights and raised the stern-weights. The sky ship tipped obligingly forwards. The stud-sail was raised, the jib was tilted. They were off.

Down through the sky they sliced. The *Great Sky Whale* loomed up before them. At the last possible moment, Wind Jackal lowered the mainsail completely and came in parallel to the great carved balustrade near the stern on the starboard side. This was exactly the point where it had been agreed the *Galerider* would make its attack.

Quint gasped with delight. He'd never witnessed his father sailing with greater precision. The *Galerider* closed in on the *Great Sky Whale*. Wind Jackal marshalled his crew.

'Stave-hooks and tolley-ropes,' he bellowed. 'Advance party, prepare to board.'

All round the gargantuan league ship the scene was repeated as the grappling-hooks of the sky pirate ships flew across the divide, found their target and held fast – to the bows, the aftcastle, the hull-rigging, the masts. And at the individual captains' command the first wave of sky pirates scrambled aboard.

They found the deck deserted. Could the league ship be completely unguarded?

All at once a horn sounded and the doors at the top of the deck-stairs burst open with a resounding crash. A phalanx of hammerhead goblins strode out on deck. The swoosh and jangle of swords, scythes and daggers being drawn filled the air. For a moment there was an eerie silence as the disbelieving sky pirates stood rooted to the spot. Suddenly, the hammerheads threw back their heads and, with one voice, gave a high-pitched scream of rage and hurled themselves at the invaders.

The next moment, all was sound and fury. Clashing metal and splintering wood. Blade-thrust and hammer-blow. Banging, thudding, screaming.

Quint strained at the balustrade, his heart thumping, as the ghastly scene unfolded before his eyes. On the poop-deck, Grim and Grem – the great cloddertrog twins – were fighting back to back, surrounded by a dozen screaming hammerhead guards swinging their evil daggers and serrated-edged swords. There was a deafening clang of metal on metal as the cloddertrogs' studded clubs struck the crescent-shaped shields of the goblins.

Above them, at the helm, a desperate battle was developing between the boarding party from the *Windspinner* and a group of hammerheads led by a huge battle-scarred veteran in a plumed helmet. Two, three, four sky pirates fell to his fearsome sword. The others dropped back in disarray.

Elsewhere on the sky ship, Quint could see the battle was going equally badly for the pirates. If a single company of hammerhead goblins could wreak such havoc, he thought, then with a full guard on board, the league ship would be impregnable.

Then, just as it looked as if the sky pirates were staring defeat in the face, the hammerheads seemed to lose heart. Was it the casualties they'd sustained? Or was it that they could see the second wave of sky pirates preparing to board?

As the battle on board hung in the balance, several of the sky pirate ships detached themselves to attack the league ship at other points. The *Fogscythe* flew up above the level of the deck and, with the great curved blades at its prow, began severing the ropes that held the sails in place. The *Thundercrusher* hovered above the aftcastle, swinging its great pendulous wrecking-ball into the wooden structure with loud, splintering crashes. While the *Windspinner* – its braziers bubbling with boiling woodtar – catapulted the scalding black pitch down onto the first of the league ship's flight-rocks.

From the *Galerider*, Quint watched it all; white-knuckled, unblinking. The second wave of sky pirates who were now boarding had definitely tipped the balance. Wherever he looked, the hammerhead guards were in retreat, disappearing down into the depths of the sky ship. With cries of victory, the sky pirates pursued them.

'Come on,' Steg Jambles said to Quint. 'Let's join them!'

Quint hesitated; his father's words rang in his ears. *Maybe with the second wave.* This *was* the second wave, after all. And there was Pen, the gangly youth, crossing onto the league ship from the *Cloudbreaker*. If *he* was allowed to board . . .

Steg climbed up onto the balustrade and jumped across the gap to the league ship. 'Well?' he called back. 'Are you coming?'

Quint glanced round the deck of the *Galerider*. Wind Jackal was nowhere to be seen. 'Yes,' he said. 'Yes, I am!' He seized a rope hanging down from the sail crossbeam above his head – still loose after the turbulent–fog – and swung across to the deck of the *Great Sky Whale*.

'Good lad,' said Steg. 'We'll make a sky pirate out of you yet.'

'This way!' bellowed a voice.

Quint turned to see a flat-head sky pirate rallying half a dozen others round him, and setting off down below deck.

'That's my old mucker, Hogmutt,' said Steg. 'Let's follow him.'

Without giving it a second thought, the pair of them set off. Through the narrow doorway they went and down the stairs. One flight. Two flights . . . Quint looked round. There wasn't a hammerhead goblin in sight.

As they reached the second quarter-landing, he heard a low hum of muffled voices; pitiful groans, sighs, wails. He turned, and there through the narrow opening before him was a terrible scene. Two hundred, maybe more, skeletal figures – mobgnomes, gnokgoblins, woodtrolls and cloddertrogs – sat chained to a central iron bolt-shaft, each one gripping a rope attached to the upper spar of a giant set of bellows. Down they pulled it, and the furnace-heated air whistled along the giant pipes that led to the flight-rocks. With a creak, the bellows sprang back. The slaves grunted with effort as they pulled the ropes back down again. Up. Down. Up. Down. Relentlessly . . .

'What is this?' gasped Quint.

'These are the underdeckers,' said Steg. 'Slaves, every one of them, condemned to warming the huge flight-rocks which keep this accursed vessel afloat. If the bellows were to stop, the rocks would cool and the *Great Sky Whale* would hurtle.'

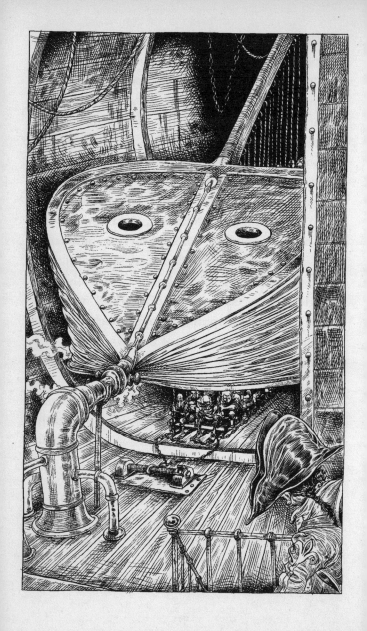

'Hurtle!' exclaimed Quint.

It was the term every sky sailor dreaded. As they all knew, since cold rock rises and hot rock sinks, skysailing depended on controlling the temperature of the flight-rock. Untended, a cooling flight-rock became increasingly buoyant and – out of control – hurtled upwards into open sky, taking its sky ship with it.

'Over here,' yelled Hogmutt, dashing off down a broad wood-panelled corridor.

They turned from the toiling slaves. 'Quick,' said Steg, seizing Quint by the arm. 'He must have discovered the treasure.'

They found him in front of a low arched door. ''Cording to that Pen character,' he was saying, 'this should be the treasury-room.'

'Then what are we waiting for?' shouted Steg Jambles. 'Smash the door down.'

Hogmutt stepped back, lowered his shoulder and rammed the door. There was a loud thud – but the door didn't budge. A swarthy brogtroll from the *Windspinner* stepped forward.

'Let me try,' he said.

There was a second, louder, thud. Still the door did not move. The sky pirates drew their clubs and cudgels and were about to batter it down when Quint spoke up.

'Are you sure it's locked?' he said.

Steg Jambles strode up to the door and tried the handle. It opened with a creak.

'I don't believe it,' Hogmutt groaned.

'Forget it,' said Steg Jambles. 'Let's see what's inside.'

One by one the group of sky pirates went in. They found themselves in a large dark room shot with beams of light from the high portholes and containing a collection of caskets and chests. Quint stared at them, his heart thumping.

'Do you think this is the treasure?' he said.

'Only one way to find out,' said Steg.

They crossed the room. Quint pulled the lid of a chest open, and gasped. It was half-full with gold and silver, and jewels that sparkled like multi-coloured

fire. And, from the yelps of surprise and delight from the rest of the room, it was clear that the other chests the sky pirates had examined were the same.

'Wealth beyond our wildest dreams,' Hogmutt bellowed, and a cheer went round.

'So, the rats have nibbled at the bait,' roared a voice.

The sky pirates spun round to see Marl Mankroyd, the Leaguesmaster himself, standing in the doorway.

'It's a trap!' Steg hissed in Quint's ear. 'Quick, lad!' He held open the treasure chest. Quint jumped inside and closed the lid.

'Pi-rats!' Marl Mankroyd sneered. And as he chuckled at his own joke, two dozen armed hammerhead goblins appeared behind him. 'Guards, seize them! Disarm them and tie them up – but do not kill them.' He smiled unpleasantly. 'You are to be executed back in Undertown as an example to others, to put an end to this accursed sky piracy once and for all.'

The room filled with hammerhead goblin guards armed to the teeth. The pirates were trapped like piebald rats in an Undertown sewer. They dropped their weapons and were immediately seized and roughly bound and gagged.

Curled up on the bed of jewels, Quint listened to the Leaguesmaster barking orders. 'Tighten those ropes! Gather up their weapons! And when you've finished, I want you back up on deck!'

Soon, it fell silent. And in the darkness of his confined hiding-place, Quint trembled with fear, waiting to make his move – wondering what that move should be.

You've been stupid and careless, he told himself. You've walked straight into an ambush. You should have guessed. You should have known . . .

On the upper-deck of the *Galerider* Wind Jackal

was muttering the self-same words to himself. All around the horizon – and closing in fast – were league ships. Thirty of them at least.

Wind Jackal chewed his lower lip, shuddered, and cursed. It had all been too easy. He should have known. He should have stopped the second wave from boarding the *Great Sky Whale*, cut his losses and made a dash for it. But now it was too late. He looked across at the helm where his son had last stood, taking the wheel.

'Quint,' he whispered, 'where *are* you?'

. CHAPTER FOUR .

THE SKY BATTLE

There was turmoil and confusion in the sky pirate fleet as the league patrol ships drew nearer. One after the other, individual sky pirate captains decided to abort the attack and flee, even if it meant abandoning some of their finest fighters. Within minutes, the fragile union of the pirate fleet had collapsed and Ice Fox had bellowed his final order down his megaphone – 'Everyone for himself!'

Wind Jackal was desperate. He sent Ramrock to scour every inch of the *Galerider* for his son. The last of the other sky pirate ships were departing as the first patrol ships came close enough to fire sky-harpoons and cannon-rocks. Wind Jackal raised his telescope to his eye to get a closer look at the attackers.

'Ruptus Pentephraxis,' he growled a moment later, as he focused in on the figure at the helm of the lead ship. 'I might have known!' And he slapped his forehead angrily as he finally remembered where he'd seen 'Pen', the gangly youth, before.

Once, when he and Ruptus Pentephraxis had fought a duel on a sky raft high over the Mire, he'd been lurking in the shadows behind the leaguesman and, when Wind Jackal had begun to get the upper hand, had fled to get help. But his name was not Pen. It was Ulbus. Ulbus Pentephraxis, for he was Ruptus's son – a vicious individual with a growing reputation for murder and assassination. At the time, Wind Jackal had left Ruptus with a small scar – and both he and his son with a huge grudge.

Ramrock came dashing up the stairs to the helm. 'Quint is nowhere to be found,' he panted.

'Oh, Quint!' Wind Jackal bellowed, with rage and fear.

'I saw him, captain,' Spillins called down from the caternest. 'Aboard the *Sky Whale*. He and Steg Jambles took the aftcastle stairs down below deck.'

Wind Jackal glanced across at the league ship to see that there were guards there now, minding the stairway. He saw something else too. Grim and Grem were sprawled out across the rear of the deck. They looked as identical in death as they had in life. Wind Jackal groaned. His two best fighters had been killed. There was nothing for it. He couldn't leave. He would have to board the *Great Sky Whale* himself to rescue his son.

'Ramrock!' he called to the stone pilot. 'Take the helm. And be prepared for a quick getaway when I return.'

He looked down over the balustrade at the mid-section of the aftcastle. It was here that the officers' quarters were usually situated – luxurious chambers with carved beds, thick carpets and heavy curtains at their large, oval portholes. As the battle raged on, and the patrol fleet closed in, Wind Jackal launched himself off the side of the *Galerider*.

His parawings clicked open and he leaned forwards, tipping the wings to one side and gliding down through the air in a wide spiral. A porthole came closer. He tugged the wings down and swung round until his feet were out in front.

'Down a tad more,' he muttered, 'and . . .'

Smash!

Wind Jackal hurtled through the glass, landed heavily on the floor and rolled over. He picked himself up and looked round.

'Bullseye!' he exclaimed.

In his hiding-place inside the treasure chest, Quint pushed the lid up and peeked out through the crack. Apart from the low murmur of conversation, it was quiet down in the hold. Six sky pirates were lying in a row, bound and gagged behind the treasure chests. Two hammerhead guards, dressed up in their armour of heavy breastplates and helmets, had been left inside the chamber to watch over the prisoners, while a third – Quint had overheard – had been put on the locked door outside.

The two hammerheads inside were sitting on caskets by the door. 'All this treasure just lying here,' one of them was saying. 'I'm sure they wouldn't miss a few gold pieces. Or a couple of gems . . .'

'No point,' said the second guard. 'They're all fake.'

'Fake?' the first said, shocked. He stood up from the casket and lifted the lid. At the same time, Quint slipped out of his chest, dropped to the floor and lowered the lid silently. 'Are you sure it's fake?' the guard was saying.

'Glass and ironwood, the lot of it,' the second guard confirmed. 'Specially made for the ambush.'

The first guard bent over, retrieved a golden coin and bit it. '*Puh . . . puh . . .*' he spluttered, and spat the splinters from his mouth.

'Told you!' said the second guard triumphantly.

Quint slithered across the floor – keeping behind the barrels and boxes – and on towards the shadows in the corner where Steg Jambles, Hogmutt and the others lay.

'The only real treasure on board is up in the Leaguesmaster's chamber,' the guard continued.

Silently, Quint reached the bound sky pirates. He slipped his knife from the sheath on his belt and sliced through the ropes at Steg's wrists and ankles. Steg wriggled free, tore off his gag and began undoing his neighbour's knots. Within seconds, all six of the sky pirates were free.

As the ropes round Hogmutt's legs came loose, his boot knocked against one of the treasure chests.

'What was that?' the two flat-heads asked one another.

'It was *this*!' roared Steg Jambles as he leapt from the shadows and hurled a casket at the startled guards.

As it struck the heavy-set goblins full in the face, it exploded into shards of splintered wood and a shower of fake jewels and coins. The guards crashed to the floor.

'See to them,' said Steg. 'I . . .' There was a grating noise as the key slid into the lock. Steg raised his hand for hush. Hogmutt picked up one of the guards' discarded swords, moved behind the door and lifted his arm, ready.

The handle slowly turned. The hinges creaked, then – *BANG* – the door suddenly flew back – missing Hogmutt by a hair's breadth. Quint stared. There in the doorway was a figure with his foot raised and his sword drawn, a hammerhead guard unconscious at his feet.

'Father!' he exclaimed then, remembering what he'd done, he dropped his head. 'I . . . I'm sorry.'

'Never mind that now,' said Wind Jackal, stepping into the room. 'We've got to get out of here, and fast. The patrol ships are closing in all round.' He hesitated. 'And this whole sky ship's crawling with hammerhead guards.'

He looked round, rapidly assessing the situation. Three unconscious guards, eight sky pirates . . .

'Tie them up,' he ordered. 'Quint, Jambles, put on the hammerheads' breastshields and helmets.'

'But why . . .?' Quint began.

'Just do as I say!' Wind Jackal growled.

The sky pirates made their way back up the staircases in a long line. Quint, Steg Jambles and Wind Jackal himself were dressed up as guards, the rest of the sky pirates were their prisoners.

As they passed the third landing, Wind Jackal glanced at his son. 'That's where I got in,' he said nodding towards an opened door. Quint looked into the room. There was broken glass all over the carpet. 'Marl Mankroyd's personal chamber,' Wind Jackal added.

Quint hesitated. 'Is it?' he said. There was a small, ornate chest at the end of the four-poster bed, and the guard's words came back to him – *the only real treasure on board is up in the Leaguesmaster's chamber.* 'Wait, Father,' said Quint. 'There's something you should know . . .'

Five minutes later, as they continued up the stairs, all the sky pirates' pockets were stuffed full of precious black diamonds – the contents of the now empty chest.

At the second quarter-landing, Wind Jackal motioned them to be still for a moment. 'Turn right at the top of the stairs,' he instructed them in a gruff whisper. 'Do not stop until we reach the *Galerider*. Ramrock should have lowered it down beneath the bulge of the *Sky Whale*'s hull and run up the white flag. They'll think she's surrendered.' He looked round. 'And if anyone challenges us, I'll do the talking. All right?'

A chorus of grunted assent went round.

'Let's go,' he said.

'Father,' Quint said urgently. 'The slaves! We must free them!'

Wind Jackal turned and saw the great bellows with the wretched underdeckers chained into position below them – even now continuing to tend to the flight-rocks. A mixture of emotions crossed his face: pity, anger, disgust. 'You're right, Quint,' he said. 'We must free them. But be warned, all of you. Once the flight-rocks are untended, this ship will begin to hurtle. We will have five minutes at most to escape.'

'And the slaves?' said Quint.

'I'll take care of that,' said Wind Jackal.

He strode over to the massed rows of toiling slaves, chained as they were to the central bolt-shaft. He struck the main bolt a mighty blow with his sword. The metal buckled, the wood splintered and the chains jangled down through the stifling air.

'Friends!' Wind Jackal announced. 'You are free. Make for the sky rafts and save yourselves. We'll buy you time to escape.' He turned back to the sky pirates. 'Come!' he bellowed. 'We must hurry.'

Shouting out their heartfelt thanks, the slaves rushed down to the lower decks where the sky rafts were secured. Wind Jackal and the others made their way to the upper decks, picking their way through the debris and the dead. All round them – both on deck and up in the sky – the fighting had subsided, and the decks were crowded with the many hammerhead goblins who had been waiting to ambush the sky pirates.

It was a well-sprung trap, thought Wind Jackal bitterly. Thank Sky, most of the pirates had already escaped. Now it was their turn.

Wind Jackal caught sight of the top of the *Galerider*'s caternest poking up above the balustrade, and they were just heading towards it when, all at once, a furious voice ripped through the air.

'Where are you taking those prisoners?'

Wind Jackal looked up. Two heavy-set guard captains were standing on the deck above them, hands on hips.

'They're to be sky-fired,' Wind Jackal replied.

'By whose orders?' one of the guards demanded.

'By the orders of the Leaguesmaster himself,' Wind Jackal stated boldly.

Marl Mankroyd appeared from behind the guards, the treacherous 'Pen' by his side. 'I've ordered no sky-firing,' he hissed. 'Come here, the three of you. Explain yourselves.'

'What do we do now?' Quint asked his father under his breath.

Suddenly the *Galerider*, with Ramrock at the helm, reared up behind them, and came in level with the deck of the *Great Sky Whale*.

'Run!' bellowed Wind Jackal.

The first of the sky pirates vaulted over the balustrade and on to the *Galerider*. The hammerhead guards drew their scythe-like swords with an evil hiss, and bore down on the rest of the sky pirates. Wind Jackal and Steg Jambles fell back to meet them.

Quint leapt on board the *Galerider* and, landing with a heavy thud, had the wind knocked out of him. He looked back. Steg and his father were battling valiantly with four guards. With a start, he saw, coming in from the east, the lead league ship with the fearsome Ruptus Pentephraxis at its helm. A great spike protruded from its prow. Any second now it would spear the *Galerider* and fix it to the *Great Sky Whale* like a butterfly pinned to a board.

'Come on!' Quint bellowed to his father. 'Now! Or you'll get cut off!'

'Let's go!' Wind Jackal shouted to Steg Jambles and the pair of them spun round, made a dash for the edge of the deck and leapt across to the *Galerider*.

The moment they landed, it soared upwards into the sky under Ramrock's expert touch. Just in time, for beneath them there was a tremendous *CRASH*! as Ruptus Pentephraxis's league ship – unable either to slow down or change course – rammed the *Great Sky Whale*, its great spike shattering the rear of the starboard hull and sending vast chunks of splintered wood from both sky ships tumbling down through the air.

From the swiftly retreating *Galerider* came the sound of cheering and jeering. They'd escaped. They'd stolen the Leaguesmaster's treasure. As for the slaves, even now, the sky rafts were flying free from the juddering *Sky Whale* – its cooling flight-rocks already straining in their cages, pulling the great vessel upwards.

Then all at once, with a creaking groan, the huge ship suddenly hurtled upwards, taking the hammerhead guards and its captain with it and disappearing beyond the clouds into open sky.

Quint punched the air. The enemy leaguesmen had been defeated; the wicked *Great Sky Whale*, destroyed. They had won the battle! A sky pirate's life didn't get much better than this!

. CHAPTER FIVE .

NAMED

It was late afternoon. The sky pirates had been celebrating since daybreak. Far in the distance, the glittering towers and spires of Sanctaphrax had finally come into view. Quint was standing at the helm with his father, Wind Jackal. Despite the upbeat rowdiness of the rest of the crew, he was in a reflective mood.

'The whole incident shows just how quickly and unpredictably grave situations can arise,' he was saying to Quint. 'Grim and Grem both dead . . .'

'Sky take their spirits,' Quint murmured.

Wind Jackal turned to him. 'Yet you did well, my son,' he said. 'Very well – despite your disobedience!'

'I said I was sorry,' said Quint quietly. 'And it wasn't all my fault anyway. If Ice Fox hadn't been deceived and . . .'

'I know, I know,' said Wind Jackal, resting his hand on his son's shoulder. 'Yet it was a close shave for all that. I was lucky this time. One day I might not be so lucky . . .'

'But Father . . . ' Quint protested.

'Let me finish, Quint,' Wind Jackal told him. 'If anything should happen to me, you will become master of the *Galerider* and then you will need a sky pirate name.' He paused. 'I will give it to you now,' he said and squeezed Quint's shoulder. 'You've earned it.'

'A sky pirate name?' said Quint. 'But don't sky pirates choose their own names when they become captains?'

'Some of the newer upstarts do,' said Wind Jackal scornfully. 'But traditional pirate families do things differently. We always have. For us, sky piracy is in the blood, and our names are handed down through the generations. My father gave me my name. Now it is time for me to give you yours. But remember, until you become the master of your own ship, it is a secret name – a name it would be unfitting for you to reveal to anyone.'

'I shan't,' Quint promised. 'But what is the name you have chosen?'

Wind Jackal came closer. He looked round, then spoke two words loud and clear into his son's ear. 'Cloud Wolf.'

'Cloud Wolf,' Quint whispered reverently.

'That's right,' said Wind Jackal. 'And that is the

last time you must utter the name before it is time
for you to use it.'

Quint nodded.

'And now,' said Wind Jackal, returning to the
flight-levers, 'we must hurry if we are not to be late
for our appointment with my old friend, Linius
Pallitax, back in Sanctaphrax.' He raised the sails
and re-aligned the hull-weights for maximum
speed.

'I wonder what he wants of us?' said Quint.

'I don't know,' said Wind Jackal, 'but when the

Most High Academe of Sanctaphrax summons you to his palace, it must be a matter of the greatest importance.'

'A new adventure!' whispered Quint.

'Yes,' said Wind Jackal, looking out across the broad sky. 'Perhaps the greatest adventure yet.'

THE END

Find out what happens when Wind Jackal and
Quint arrive in Sanctaphrax in . . .

THE CURSE OF THE GLOAMGLOZER

The Edge Chronicles

by Paul Stewart and Chris Riddell

High over the sprawling city
of Undertown, the academics
of the Edgeworld carry out
their studies in the floating city
of Sanctaphrax. A place full of
treachery and intrigue, Quint
helps the Most High Academe
and his daughter, Maris, with a
series of dangerous and very
secret experiments. It is to lead
Quint into an adventure deep
within the stonecomb of the
rock, in the twisting tunnels
and eerie shadows leading to
the heart-rock itself – and to
an encounter with the most
dangerous creature known
to the Edgeworld . . .

*Coming in Doubleday hardback
in Autumn 2001*

If you enjoyed *Cloud Wolf*, you will also enjoy
reading the other titles in *The Edge Chronicles*:

BEYOND THE DEEPWOODS

Book One in The Edge Chronicles

Paul Stewart & Chris Riddell

'Your destiny lies beyond the Deepwoods . . .'

Abandoned at birth in the perilous Deepwoods, Twig is
brought up by a family of
woodtrolls. One cold night, Twig
does what no woodtroll has ever
done before – *he strays from the path.*

So begins a heart-stopping
adventure that will take Twig
through a nightmare world of
goblins and trogs, bloodthirsty
beasts and flesh-eating trees. One
desire alone drives Twig on: the
longing to discover his true identity
and his destiny . . .

Created by an exciting new writing
team, this compelling fantasy, with
its brilliantly witty illustrations, is
set to become a future classic.

SHORTLISTED FOR THE LANCASHIRE
CHILDREN'S BOOK AWARD

ISBN: 0 552 545929

STORMCHASER

Book Two in The Edge Chronicles
Paul Stewart & Chris Riddell

*'It's the Great Storm,' the captain roared . . . 'We're
going stormchasing!'*

On board the *Stormchaser* is Twig, a young
crew-member drawn by destiny to join the sky
pirates, filled with excitement at the adventure
ahead.

Their quest is to collect *stormphrax* – a valuable
substance created inside the heart of the Storm,
at the very instant it unleashes its
most intense power. But only
a sky ship such as the
Stormchaser, captained by
the great Cloud Wolf,
could risk entering the
Storm . . .

The second title in
The Edge Chronicles,
a thrilling fantasy
series filled with
memorable characters
and wonderfully witty
illustrations.

ISBN: 0 552 546283

MIDNIGHT OVER SANCTAPHRAX

Book Three in The Edge Chronicles

Paul Stewart & Chris Riddell

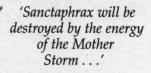

'Sanctaphrax will be destroyed by the energy of the Mother Storm . . .'

Far over the Edge, a mighty storm is brewing – a whirling vortex of immense power and unimaginable ferocity that is essential to the survival of the Edgelands . . .

In its path is Sanctaphrax – a magnificent city built on a floating rock and tethered to the land by a massive chain . . .

Only Twig – a young sky pirate captain who has dared to sail over the Edge – has learned of the approaching danger. But the perilous voyage destroys his sky ship, hurling his crew far into – and beyond – the Deepwoods, robbing Twig of all memory . . .

Midnight over Sanctaphrax can be read as a single action-packed adventure or as the final triumphant tale in a magnificent trilogy of tales about Twig, son of Cloud Wolf.

Available in Doubleday hardback:
ISBN 0 385 600895

Coming in Corgi paperback in Autumn 2001

ABOUT THE AUTHORS

PAUL STEWART is a well-established author of books for young readers – everything from picture books to football stories, fantasy and horror. Several of his books are published by Transworld, including *The Wakening*, which was selected as a Pick of the Year by the Federation of Children's Book Groups.

CHRIS RIDDELL is an accomplished graphic artist who has illustrated many acclaimed books for children, including *Something Else* by Kathryn Cave (Viking), which was shortlisted for the Kate Greenaway Medal and the Smarties Prize and won the Unesco Award. *The Swan's Stories* by Brian Alderson (Walker Books) was shortlisted for the 1997 Kurt Maschler Award and, in 2000, *Castle Diary* (Walker Books) was also shortlisted for the Kate Greenaway Award.

**All Transworld titles are available by post
from:**

Book Service By Post, PO Box 29,
Douglas, Isle of Man, IM99 1BQ

Credit cards accepted.
Please telephone 01624 836000, fax 01624 837033
or Internet http://www.bookpost.co.uk
or e-mail: bookshop@enterprise.net for details

Free postage and packing in the UK.
Overseas customers: allow £1 per book
(paperbacks) and £3 per book (hardbacks).